Firebird

he lived for the sunshine

Story by
**Brent McCorkle
and Amy Parker**

Illustrations by
**Rob Corley
and Chuck Vollmer**

KIDS

Nashville, Tennessee

Text and illustrations © 2012 Free to Love, LLC.

Published in 2012 by B&H Publishing Group,

Nashville, Tennessee

ISBN: 978-1-4336-7917-9

Dewey Decimal Classification: 231.6
Subject Heading: GOD—FICTION \ LOVE—FICTION \ BIRDS—FICTION

1 2 3 4 5 6 7 8 • 16 15 14 13 12

*Dedicated to all of those
serving at-risk children,
for showing them sunshine
through the storms.*

Once upon a time,
there lived a
little baby oriole . . .

. . . named *Firebird*.
His mama named him that on account of
his brilliantly beautiful orange feathers.

*F*irebird just *lived* for the sunshine.
On those glorious sunny days,
he would fly way up high,
to the highest branch he could find,
throw back his little head,
and bask in the glow of the sun.

But, oh, when the rains came,
little Firebird would whine and complain.
"Why, Mama?" he'd ask. "Why does
God let the storm take the sun away?"

Mama would just smile and say,
"You'll know someday, baby."
Then she'd get that faraway look, as if
she were looking straight up to the sun.
"You'll know, when you take
a walk on the clouds."

Now, over and over again the rains would come, and over and over again Firebird would complain to his mama.

Until one day,
a huge storm rolled in,
and Mama had a
different answer.

"Firebird," Mama said with a nod toward the clouds, "the answers are up there waitin' for you. But you're gonna have to fly on up there and see it for yourself."

Little Firebird was so scared.

He hadn't used his wings much at all!

And now they trembled at the sight

of the storm clouds above.

Still, he just had to find out for himself.

He had to know why God let the

storm take the sun away.

So up, up, up he went,

up into the great unknown.

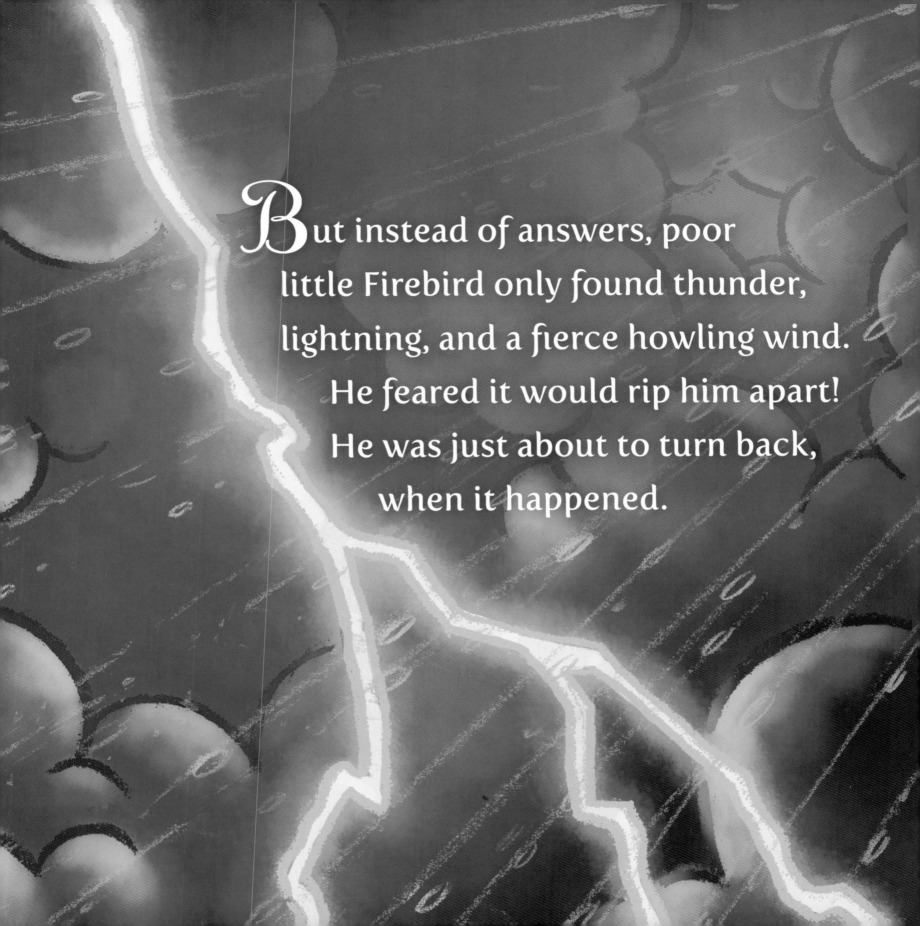

But instead of answers, poor little Firebird only found thunder, lightning, and a fierce howling wind. He feared it would rip him apart! He was just about to turn back, when it happened.

Firebird broke through the clouds.
And there it was.
In that one moment,
it all became clear.

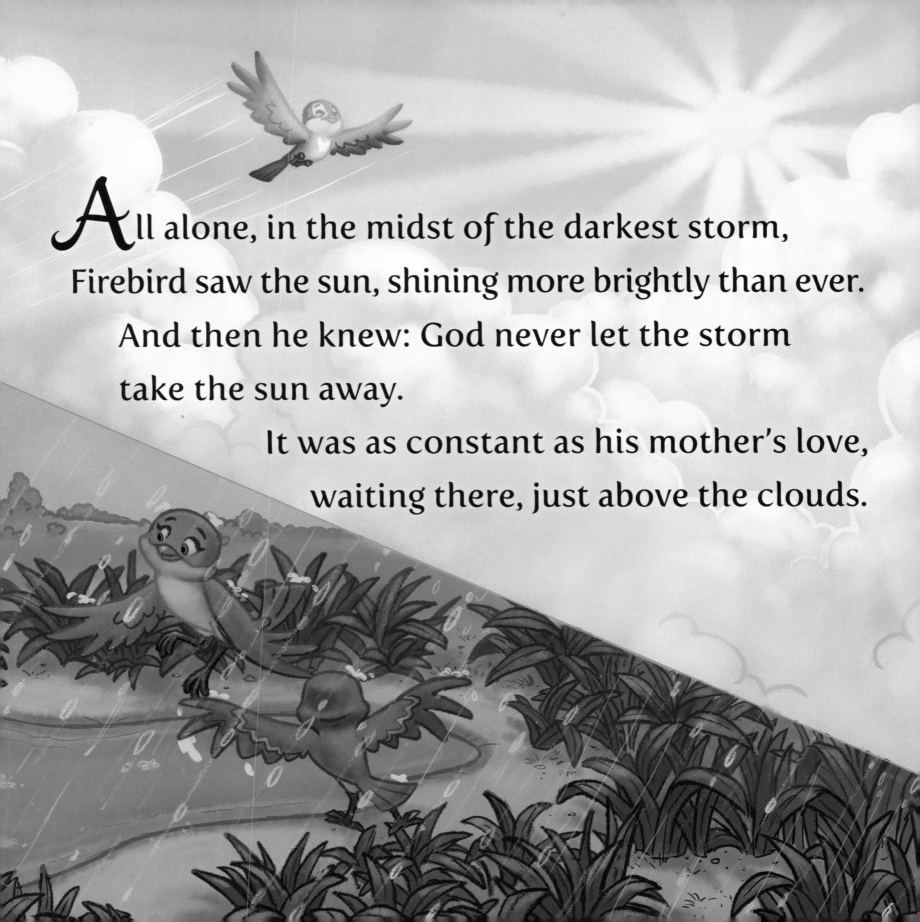

All alone, in the midst of the darkest storm,
Firebird saw the sun, shining more brightly than ever.
And then he knew: God never let the storm
take the sun away.

It was as constant as his mother's love,
waiting there, just above the clouds.

Little Firebird never forgot that moment (even after he was a big Firebird).

He still loved to bask in the sunshine.
But more importantly,
   knowing the sun was always there,
      Firebird had learned to rejoice in the rain.